This book belongs to

---- --

and I like to play

---- --

"Tig!"

First published in Great Britain 2003
by Egmont Books Limited
239 Kensington High Street
London W8 6SA

To Eilis,
Emilie and Peter
J.T.

To Miss Russell,
and all in Class 1
A.B.

NEWCASTLE UPON TYNE
CITY LIBRARIES

C3 435616 OO 72	
Askews	Oct-2003
	£4.99

Text copyright © Janet Thomas 2003

Illustrations copyright © Alison Bartlett 2003

ISBN 1 4052 0597 0

10 9 8 7 6 5 4 3 2 1

Printed in Italy

Janet Thomas and Alison Bartlett have asserted their moral rights. A CIP catalogue record for this title is available from The British Library

Can I Play?

Janet Thomas
illustrated by Alison Bartlett

Casper Cat and Susie Sheep were **best friends**.
They played **everything** together.

Unless . . .

. . . Milly Goat was there.
If Milly was there, Susie and Milly played together
and Casper was **left on his own**.

Milly liked to play tig.
Casper said, "Can I play?"
But Milly said, "**No**,
tig is for **two**.
You can't play."

So Casper had to watch.

When it was just Casper and Susie, they played houses . . .

and vets . . .

and shops . . .

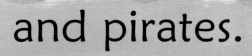

and pirates.

But when Milly came along she said,
"We're playing tig."
Casper said, "Can I play?"

Milly said, "**No**,
tig is for **two**.
You can't play."

So Casper had to watch.

One day, Casper's mummy took him to the park.
There was a **big crowd** and they were
all playing tig.
"Can I play?" he said.

"Yes, if you want," said Dan Dog.

So Casper did.
He played tig **all** morning and it was the
most fun he'd had in ages.

The next day, Casper was **really excited**.
When Susie and Milly started to play tig
he said, "Can I play?"
But Milly said, "**No**, **tig** is for **two**."
"**It isn't**," said Casper. "I played it in the park.
Let me show you."

"No!"
Milly shouted.
"Tig is only for **two**.
**You
can't
play!"**

Casper ran inside.
He told his mummy **everything**.

His mummy gave him a big cuddle.
"Let's see what we can
do," she said.

The next day, Casper's mummy took Casper **and** Milly and Susie to the park.

Everyone was playing tig.

"Come on," said Casper to Milly and Susie.
"Let's play tig!"

"No!"
Milly shouted.
"Tig is for TWO!   YOU

Everyone stared at Milly.
Casper took a big breath
and shouted,
"YES I CAN!"

And Casper went off to play . . .

. . . while Milly and Susie watched.

Casper played **all** morning. Not just Tig.
He showed the children how to play
pirates . . .

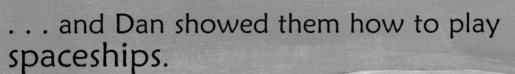

. . . and Dan showed them how to play
spaceships.

But **all** the games were better . . .

. . . when **everybody** played!

A note from the author and illustrator

Janet says,

"In primary school, we had a game called 'mush', which was very like tig, but played on three manhole covers in the playground. They were safe if you were on them, but if anyone shouted 'mush', you had to run for another, while the person who was 'on' tried to tig you. It was basically shouting and running a lot, and I loved it."

Janet aged 3 in her shop

Alison making silly faces with her son, Joel

Alison says,

"When I was young I also played this game, but at my school it was called 'drain touch'. I didn't like it much. Someone always fell over and grazed their knee. And that person was usually me!"